The Case of the Spoiled Rotten Spy

by James Preller
illustrated by Jamie Smith
cover illustration by R. W. Alley

A
LITTLE APPLE
PAPERBACK

SCHOLASTIC INC.
New York   Toronto   London   Auckland   Sydney
Mexico City   New Delhi   Hong Kong   Buenos Aires

Read all the Jigsaw Jones Mysteries!

And Don't Miss . . .

For the students and teachers at
Rydal Elementary School

ISBN-13: 978-0-439-89623-8
ISBN-10: 0-439-89623-1

Text copyright © 2007 by James Preller.
Illustrations copyright © 2007 by Scholastic Inc.

All rights reserved. Published by Scholastic Inc.

SCHOLASTIC, LITTLE APPLE, A JIGSAW JONES MYSTERY, and associated logos are trademarks and/or registered trademarks of Scholastic Inc.

12 11 10 9 8 7 6 5 4 3 2 1   7 8 9 10 11 12/0

Special thanks to Robin Wasserman

Printed in the U.S.A.
First printing, April 2007

CONTENTS

BE A STAR!!!
* * *
EXTRAS needed for
SPY GUY television
show.
If you are a
child, age 7-9.
We want you!
Auditions Saturday
@ 9am.
512 Sullivan Street

Chapter One

Extra, Extra, Read All About It!

My sister, Hillary, is afraid of three things:

Chickens.

Baked zucchini.

And zits.

So when I heard her scream, the first thing I did was look out the window. Not a chicken in sight.

I sniffed . . . pizza for dinner. Mom would *never* make zucchini pizza.

That could only mean one thing. One

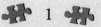

big red pimple. Probably on the tip of Hillary's nose.

I was down in the basement, and I stayed there. Teenagers are weird enough on a good day.

"*JIGSAW!*" Hillary shrieked. "Get up here!"

I took a sip of my grape juice. I added a piece to my jigsaw puzzle. And then I stood up. Nice and slow.

"*Theodore!*" Hillary shouted. Uh-oh. That was a bad sign. No one ever calls me Theodore except my mom.

"I'm coming," I grumbled. I trudged up the stairs.

Yeesh.

Hillary handed me a bright red piece of paper. "They're all over town," she squealed.

I read the flyer:

BE A STAR!!!

★ ★ ★

Extras needed for SPY GUY television show.

If you are a child, ages 7–9,

We want YOU!

Auditions Saturday @ 9 A.M.,
512 Sullivan Street

"So?" I said.

"So?" she repeated loudly. *"So?!"*

"Yeah." I shrugged. "So what?"

Hillary's eyes bugged out. "Soooo, *Spy Guy* is filming in our town. It's *the* hottest show on TV."

I shrugged again. I'd seen it. Some kid ran around with fake spy gear pretending to solve crimes. Big deal. I'm a *real* detective.

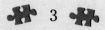

I've uncovered buried treasure, rescued a stolen bicycle, and found a lost frog. Who needs some TV detective when you've got the real thing?

"They're hiring extras, Jigsaw," Hillary screeched. "Regular people like you and me can be on the show. We could be famous!"

"Uh, did you say 'we'?" I asked.

Hillary jabbed her finger at the flyer.

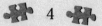

"They're looking for children, ages seven to nine. That's you. I'll take you to the audition. Then they'll meet *me*. Once they hear about all the acting I've done, they might give me a chance!"

"But I don't *want* to audition," I said. "I've got better things to do on a Saturday morning. Like trim my toenails."

Hillary narrowed her eyes. "I'll do your chores for a week."

How could I say no to that?

Chapter Two

A Star Is Bored

The next day, Hillary woke me early. She had already been up for hours. She said she had tried on four outfits already. Go figure.

I threw on a T-shirt. Pulled on my baseball cap. And I was good to go.

We got there early, so we'd be first in line. Great thinking, right? Except everyone else had the same idea.

Sullivan Street was a mess. Bright yellow police tape blocked off the road. People with walkie-talkies filled the sidewalks. The street was packed with green trailers

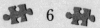

marked STAR CARS. Hillary explained they were for the cast and crew. Some of them had couches, kitchens, and even TVs inside.

I yawned.

A bunch of kids from my school stood under a big sign that read: EXTRAS. They were waiting in a line that stretched around the block. At the front of it sat a woman with spiky pink hair.

"That must be the casting director," Hillary whispered. "She's in charge of picking the actors. How do I look?"

"It's easy. You just open your eyes," I joked.

Hillary glared at me. Then she hurried away, muttering something about rotten little brothers.

I got in line. Too bad my best friend, Mila, wasn't around. But she had a piano lesson.

I wondered if it was too late to take up the kazoo.

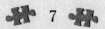 7

"Bored?" a boy asked. He was a few years older than me, and he looked sort of familiar.

"I don't love standing on line," I admitted. "But I've never seen how they make a TV show before. It's interesting."

Everywhere I looked, people ran back and forth, shouting to one another. I still didn't think being on a TV show was any big deal.

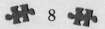 8

But I decided that *making* one might be kind of cool.

A girl suddenly exclaimed, "It's Chase! Chase Jackson!"

Chase Jackson was the star of *Spy Guy*. He was the most famous ten-year-old on the planet. And he was standing right next to me.

A bunch of star-struck kids pushed and

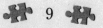

shoved to get closer to Chase, but he had disappeared.

"I saw you talking to him, Jigsaw," Lucy Hiller squealed. "What's he like?"

"He's like five feet tall," I answered. But she wasn't listening.

"It's always like that," a boy complained. "Once *he's* around, you might as well be invisible."

"Do I know you?" I asked.

The boy shook his head. His blond hair

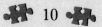

flopped into his eyes. "No one knows me. But they will. Some day. I'm Hunter Stone. I play Chase's partner in this week's episode. Are you an actor, too?"

"I'm a detective," I said proudly. "A real one." I handed him my business card:

NEED A MYSTERY SOLVED?
Call Jigsaw Jones
or Mila Yeh!
for a dollar a day,
we make problems go away
CALL 555-4523
or 555-4374

The pink-haired woman suddenly grabbed the card out of his hand.

"How cute!" She tugged at the front of my baseball cap. "You're pretending to be a detective!"

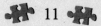

"I don't pretend," I insisted. "And I'm definitely *not* cute." You can call me a lot of things. "Worm," "Shorty," even "Theodore." But "cute" isn't one of them.

The woman didn't care. She stared me straight in the eye. "You're just what we've been looking for," she chirped. "Cute as a button. And so *real.* Congratulations, you're hired!"

Chapter Three

Lights, Camera — Disaster!

Every day after school that week, I went down to the set. That's what the TV people called the place where they were filming. I learned lots of other TV words while I was there:

A **close-up** was when the camera zoomed in on someone's face.

A **prop** was something the actors used in a scene, like a magnifying glass or a cell phone.

And a **gaffer** was the person in charge of all the electric stuff.

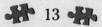

But that's not all. I learned that everyone on TV wears makeup, even the boys. Even *me*.

Yeesh.

I learned that the director, Les Lesterson, spent half his day on the phone. I learned that Chase Jackson always got the star treatment. And I learned that when your big sister says she'll never speak to you again because you stole her chance to be a star, "never" means two days.

I enjoyed the silence — while it lasted.

But here's the most important thing I learned: Making a TV show can sometimes be as exciting as waiting for Jell-O to harden.

You had to wait for the gaffer to set up the lighting. You had to wait for the director to show the actors where to stand. You had to wait for the hair, makeup, and costume people to make the actors look perfect.

Finally, it would be time to film. The director called, "Action!" and the cameras rolled. The actors said their lines. It was pretty cool.

For about fifteen seconds.

Then the director called, "Cut!" And the whole process started all over again. The endless waiting, the standing around, the fifteen seconds of excitement.

"I don't need any makeup," I told the makeup woman, Alicia K, when it was my turn in the chair. She hadn't stopped talking from the moment she arrived, which was about twenty minutes after she was supposed to be there. That was another thing I learned: Alicia K was always late.

"I like my face the way it is," I told her.

"Without makeup, you'd look pale and shiny on camera," Alicia said. She patted my face with a giant puffball. A cloud of pink powder floated into the air.

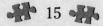

AH-CHOO!

Alicia smiled down at me. "Don't worry, honey. I'm going to make you look beautiful."

That's what I was afraid of.

I sat while Alicia powdered my face. When she was done, she asked if I wanted to look in the mirror. I shook my head.

I figured it was better not to know.

Instead, I sat down on the curb next to

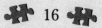

Hunter Stone. As soon as Chase arrived, we would start filming.

Or so I thought.

"Someone tore my costume!" Chase cried, storming up to the director. He was holding a pair of black pants with a tear in the cuff.

"He probably tore it himself," Hunter whispered. "But he won't get in trouble for it. Chase never gets in trouble for anything."

He was right.

Les Lesterson whirled around and pointed at Hunter. "You, kid. Go tell the costumer we've got a problem."

"But I'm an *actor*," Hunter insisted.

"That's not important. Chase wants this taken care of," the director snapped. He rolled his eyes. "And what Chase wants . . ."

". . . Chase gets," Hunter grumbled.

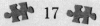 17

"Okay, let's try this again. Places, people!" the director shouted. He perched in a high chair just behind the camera.

"Lights, camera —" Les stopped suddenly. His walkie-talkie blared. He held it up to his ear, and his jaw dropped open. "Cut!" he shouted. "Someone on this set is a thief!"

Chapter Four

Caught on Film?

"The pig is gone," the director announced. Everyone gasped. Everyone except me.

"What pig?" I asked. As far as I could tell, this was a TV set, not a farm.

"It's not a real pig," Les Lesterson said. "It's a prop. This episode is about Chase's character searching for something called the Axelrod Antimatter Electro-Grav-Matic."

"The Axel-Anti-*what*?" I said.

"Exactly. That's why we call it 'the pig.'

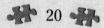

It's pink. It's kind of pig-shaped. It's important — and now it's missing!"

A guy ran over from the prop room. "We searched everywhere, Boss," he panted. "It's gone!" He handed Les Lesterson a videotape. "Here's today's security video."

"Aha!" the director cried. "Now we'll catch the thief!"

We gathered around a monitor. The director pressed PLAY. A grainy black-and-white image came up on the screen. It showed a long, narrow room filled with props. A number at the bottom marked the time: 9:31 A.M.

The director pointed to something in the corner of the screen. "There's the pig. Let's see where it went."

He hit FAST FORWARD, and the clock in the corner sped ahead. At 11:13 A.M., the door to the prop room swung open. A figure crept inside. He was dressed all in black. The figure stuffed the Axelrod Antimatter

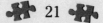

Electro-Grav-Matic under his arm, then slipped out the door. The director turned to Chase Jackson. "*You* stole it?" he asked in disbelief.

"That's not me!" Chase argued. "You can't even see that guy's face."

"It looks like you," the director pointed out. "It's your costume."

"But anyone could have been wearing it," Chase said. "Anyone like..." He looked around wildly. Then he pointed at Hunter. "Him! He's my size, and he's jealous of me."

Hunter's eyes widened. He opened his mouth, but nothing came out.

"That's impossible!" Alicia jumped in. "Hunter was in my trailer at eleven-thirteen."

"How do you know it was exactly eleven-

thirteen?" I asked. After all, Alicia *never* seemed to know what time it was.

"I remember looking at the clock just before Hunter came in, because it was almost time for *Oprah*," she said. "That's my favorite show. I watch it every day. But it was only a little after eleven, and *Oprah* starts at noon. That's when Hunter came in. He stayed for at least twenty minutes. . . ."

I got the idea. According to the witness, Alicia, Hunter was in her trailer at 11:13. He *couldn't* have stolen the pig.

Les Lesterson frowned. "Come on, Chase. Where's the pig?"

"I don't have it!" Chase insisted.

"We won't need it for a couple of days. That gives the thief" — the director glared at Chase — "some time to think about what he's done. But if that pig isn't back by the end of the week, *someone's* going to pay."

"Not me!" Chase stormed away.

I followed him around the corner. He

didn't look angry anymore. He looked worried.

"I think I can help," I told him.

"*You?*" Chase raised an eyebrow. "You're just an extra. How could *you* help *me*?"

"I'm a detective," I explained. "I don't know who stole the pig, but I can try to find out."

"Do you believe I didn't take it?" Chase asked.

I could have lied. But a detective's got

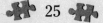

to be honest. "I don't believe in anything except the facts," I said. "Right now, I don't know what to believe."

Chase frowned. He paused for a minute. "I guess that's good enough. You're hired. When you find the rat who *did* take the pig, you'll know I'm telling the truth."

My gut told me he was right. But that wasn't good enough.

I needed proof.

Chapter Five

Normal Life

"Are you *sure* Chase didn't steal the pig?" Mila asked. We were waiting in my basement office for Chase to arrive.

"No," I admitted. "It may have been him on the security tape. It was hard to tell."

"What about the tape itself?" Mila asked. "Are you sure that was real?"

It hit me like a fly swatter. Why hadn't I seen it before? Anyone who could direct a TV show could easily make a fake security tape.

I opened my detective journal. "That gives us two suspects."

Les Lesterson
Hunter Stone

"Les doesn't seem to like Chase," I explained. "I also think Chase is right about Hunter. Hunter claims he's innocent, but he does seem jealous."

"But the witness, Alicia, says Hunter was with her at eleven-thirteen," Mila pointed out. "Is there anyone else who might want to get Chase in trouble?"

"Anyone?" I said. "Try *everyone*."

I had asked a bunch of people on the set about the missing pig. The cameraman, a lighting guy, even the stunt double. Each person had two things in common. Number one: They all said they didn't do it. Number two: They all seemed to dislike Chase Jackson.

 28

Not because they knew him, but because they didn't. They assumed he was a spoiled star. So they stayed away.

"They all think he's spoiled rotten," I said.

"Um, Jigsaw?" Mila said softly. She pointed behind me. Chase Jackson was standing in the doorway.

Oops.

A big smile stretched across Chase's face. Maybe he hadn't heard. Or maybe he was just a better actor than I thought. Either way, I felt bad. Chase *was* spoiled. But he was my client. I was supposed to stick up for the guy.

My dog, Rags, was lying in the doorway, asleep. Chase stepped over him. That's Rags for you. He's a great pet — just not much of a guard dog.

Chase glanced around. "This dump is your office?"

I pointed to the desk in the corner of my basement. The sign behind it read: JIGSAW

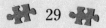 29

JONES, PRIVATE EYE. "Yeah," I grumbled. "You have a problem with that?"

"It's kind of messy," Chase complained. He sat on the edge of a chair, like he was afraid of germs. "Are you sure you're a real detective?"

"I am," I said. "If you pay me a real dollar."

Chase laughed. "I'm a TV star. You should help me for free."

"To me, you're just a regular guy," I said. "So pay up, or take a hike."

"A regular guy?" Chase paused, thinking it over. "I guess that's okay." He forked over a crisp dollar bill.

"I'm Mila. It's nice to meet you," Mila said.

"I'm sure it is," Chase said. "Do you want my autograph?"

"No, thanks," Mila said. "Let's focus on the case."

Chase nodded. "You're right. Jigsaw and I

have a lot to talk about. Could you go get me a soda?"

Mila scowled. She looked like she would love to get Chase a soda . . . and pour it on his head.

"What's wrong?" Chase asked. He turned to me. "Isn't Lila your assistant?"

"It's *Mila*," I corrected him. "And she's my *partner*."

Chase looked confused. "But what do you do when you need something?"

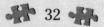

"Usually I yell, 'Mom!'" I said. "Thing is, that hasn't been working so well lately. She has an attitude problem. She says I'm old enough to get things for myself."

"Bummer," Chase noted.

"Tell me about it," I replied. "I liked it better when I could boss her around."

"Okay, guys," Mila said. "Let's get down to business."

Chapter Six

Dogcatcher

The next afternoon, I got permission for Mila to visit the set. She brought Rags with her. We hoped he might be able to sniff out the pig.

Chase came along to check out the scene of the crime. I warned him that it would be hard work. He didn't care.

"This is important," he said. "I have to find out who stole the pig. We can't film the show without it."

"But that's why you hired us," I reminded him.

"I know," Chase said. "But I want to help."

I was starting to figure out Chase Jackson. He didn't mean to act spoiled. It wasn't his fault that he thought he was the center of the world. After all, most people treated him that way.

We left Rags outside the prop room and went inside. The room looked like it did on the video. It was long and narrow, filled with props of all kinds. A lot of it was phony spy equipment. There were binoculars, telescopes, and walkie-talkies. It was a detective's paradise.

Or it would have been, if any of it were real.

Mila and I showed Chase how to search for clues. We checked every shelf and looked at every prop. We examined every inch of the floor. It was hard work. But Chase didn't complain.

Then suddenly, he shouted, "I found something!" Chase pointed to a muddy

 35

footprint. He grinned proudly. For once in his life, Chase was doing *real* detective work.

I drew a picture of the footprint in my detective notebook.

"What are you doing?" Chase asked.

"If we can match this footprint to a shoe," I explained, "we might have a new suspect."

On our way out of the prop room, we ran into Les Lesterson, the director. When Les saw Rags, he sneered. I guess he didn't like dogs.

That was too bad, because Rags liked him.

Or, at least, Rags liked the sandwich Les had in his hand.

Rags lunged for the sandwich. Les jumped backward. He ran away. Rags figured he wanted to play tag.

So Les ran left. And Rags ran left. Les

turned right. Rags raced right. Les zigged.
Rags zagged.

Les tripped and fell. Rags leaped on him
like a football player on Super Bowl Sunday.
He stuck out his big, wet tongue and jumped
toward the director's face.

SLURP!

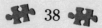

Chapter Seven
Big Spies Don't Cry

"GET THIS DOG OFF MY SET!" Les Lesterson yelled. He stood up, brushed himself off, and yelled some more. Even after Mila took Rags home, Les kept yelling. And then something strange happened.

Chase nudged me. "Watch this." He took a deep breath. He closed his eyes. And then Chase Jackson burst into tears.

I didn't know what to do. And neither did the director.

"Quit crying, kid," Les stuttered. "You want me to find your mommy?"

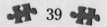 39

"No, I got stung by a bee!" Chase blubbered. "And it hurts so bad!"

"It's just a bee, kid," Les said. "You act like you lost a leg or something."

"I'm scared of bees!" Chase wailed. He pointed to a big green trailer a few feet away. The door said: DIRECTOR. "Can I hide in there until it flies away?"

"Sure. Anything to get you to stop crying." Les let us into his trailer, then hurried away. He had work to do.

When Les left, Chase instantly stopped crying. "How'd you like that?" he asked. "Pretty good, huh?"

"What?" I asked.

"I was never really *crying*," Chase explained. "That was *acting*. I wanted to get us inside the trailer."

I was impressed. It was a neat trick. When you're crying, people will do *anything* to get you to stop.

"When Les fell down, I saw the bottom of his shoes." Chase said. "It matched the footprint exactly. And if Les stole the pig, his trailer would be a good place to hide it."

Hmmm. Maybe Chase wasn't a fake spy.

We searched the trailer. It had a bathroom, two couches, a plasma television, and even a tiny kitchen. It had almost everything. Except the pig.

We found a wall of photos, each of Les Lesterson next to a different famous

person. We found a floppy stuffed bunny tucked under a couch cushion, and a recipe for carrot soup taped to the wall.

But we couldn't find a single clue linking Les to the missing pig.

Chase plopped down on the couch. "What if we never find the pig?" he asked. "They'll think I took it. What if they kick me off the show? Then I won't be a star anymore."

"We'll find the pig," I told him.

I may have sounded sure, but I wasn't.

Good thing Chase wasn't the only one who could act.

Chapter Eight

A Regular Guy

On Friday morning, I got to Room 201 a few minutes early. I dropped a folded-up note on Mila's desk.

Mila unfolded the note.

> It was very nice to meet your friend yesterday. It made me smile when she stood by the tree and made those funny faces. She has kind of a big mouth. But she laughed at all my jokes, and she plays baseball at recess. So I think she's okay.

At first, Mila wrinkled her nose in confusion. But then she caught my eye. She slid her finger across her nose. That's our secret signal. It meant she understood that the note was written in code.

Mila and I are always looking for new secret codes. The week before, we had come up with a new one. We took two pieces of paper and cut out a bunch of rectangles, in the same place on both sheets of paper.

When we were done, we had two pages that looked like this:

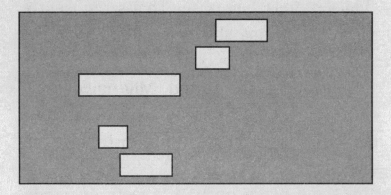

We each kept one. Those were our code breakers. When I wanted to write Mila a message, all I needed to do was lay the code breaker over a blank piece of paper. I fit my message into the empty boxes.

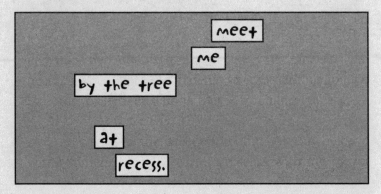

Then I took the code breaker away and I filled in a bunch of other words.

Mila pulled out her code breaker. She laid it down over my note, then she looked at me and nodded. She'd gotten the message.

During recess, I told Mila all about searching Les Lesterson's trailer. And I told her what we'd come up with: a big, fat nothing.

"Are you absolutely, positively, one-hundred-percent sure that Chase didn't take the pig himself?" Mila asked.

"Pretty sure," I said. "If he stole the pig, why would he pay us to find the real thief? And why would he steal it in the first place?"

"Why would anyone?" Mila replied. "That's the key. If we can figure out the *why*, it could lead us to the *who*."

Mila was right. *Why* was always a good question. What was the motive?

Lucy Hiller and Kim Lewis squeezed between me and Mila.

"Jigsaw, we've been looking all over for you," Lucy said. She squinted at me like she thought I'd been trying to avoid her.

I had been.

"I'm kind of busy right now," I said. "We have a very important case and —"

"This is important, too!" Lucy informed me. She smoothed down her flowered skirt and folded her arms. "I need you to tell me everything you know about Chase Jackson."

"Why?" I asked.

"Because I'm the new president of the Chase Jackson Fan Club," Lucy explained.

"And I'm vice president," Kim added eagerly.

"We're his number one, all-time biggest fans," Lucy said. "Tell me everything. What does he wear? What does he eat? What does he like to read? What kind of toothpaste does he use?"

"What's his favorite food?" Kim asked.

"And his favorite color? Does he like his peanut butter creamy or crunchy?"

"What about pets?" Lucy asked. "Does he like cats or dogs?"

"Chocolate ice cream or vanilla?" Kim continued.

I held my hands over my ears. This had been going on all week. Suddenly, I was the most popular kid in school, just because I knew a TV star.

"Why do you care so much?" I asked. "He's just a regular guy."

"*Regular?*" Kim and Lucy said together. They couldn't believe it.

"Jigsaw, he's on TV," Lucy told me. "He's *famous*. Millions and millions of people watch his show. *You* may be a regular guy. But Chase Jackson?" She got a dreamy look in her eyes. "He's a star."

They fired more questions at me, but I wasn't listening. Lucy's words were still bouncing around my head. Three words in particular:

Millions and millions.

That's how many people would be watching *me* on TV someday soon. I gulped. It sounded like a lot. I was supposed to film my scene that afternoon. I had been so busy, I had almost forgotten about it. What if I messed up?

After all, I wasn't a real actor. Like Lucy said, I was just a regular guy.

A regular guy with a bad feeling in his stomach.

Chapter Nine

On the Set

"Lights, camera, action!" the director shouted.

I stood perfectly still. All I had to do was wait for Chase to run up and ask, "Which way did he go?" That's when I was supposed to reply, "He went that way."

Easy as a three-piece jigsaw puzzle, right?

Wrong.

Chase Jackson ran up. "Which way did he go?"

I opened my mouth and —

Nothing happened.

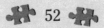

"He . . . he . . . he . . ." I stammered. I couldn't remember what came next.

"Cut!" the director shouted. "What's with the extra?"

"I'll help him," Chase said. He bent his head close to mine. "Nervous?" he whispered. I might have said yes.

"Don't look at the camera," Chase said. "Don't even think about the camera. Just look at me. Okay?"

I nodded. I would try to forget about the camera and the millions and millions of people who would watch the show. Millions and millions and millions . . .

Forget about it, I told myself. It was just one lousy line. I knew I could do it.

At least, I hoped I could.

Chase gave Les Lesterson the thumbs-up.

"Action!" the director shouted.

"He went that way," I said. Chase took off, and the director called, "Cut!" I let out a sigh of relief.

 54

"You were great!" Chase said. "Let's celebrate." He led me over to the craft services table. That's like the TV version of a snack bar. Except that this snack bar had more food than I'd ever seen in my life — and we were allowed to take as much of it as we wanted.

I was starving. Being an actor was hungry work.

I filled a plate with cookies, brownies, pretzels, chips, and cheese twists. Then I stuck a raisin on top. Just to be healthy.

Chase stuffed a chocolate doughnut hole in his mouth. "Come on, I know where we can go."

Chase led me to a small building. It looked like a secret laboratory. It was dark and spooky, stuffed with test tubes and weird gizmos. I recognized it: This was the set where Chase was supposed to first discover the pig.

We sat at a table and chowed down. Chase

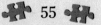

told me all about life as a big Hollywood star. I told him what it was like to be a regular kid. He said that back home, he had a swimming pool, a tennis court, and six big-screen TVs. But he wasn't allowed to have a dog, because his mother didn't want to get dog hair all over the mansion. He didn't go to a regular school, and he didn't have many friends.

I had to admit, parts of his life sounded like fun. But not as fun as having Rags.

 56

After all, a swimming pool wouldn't make a very good best friend. And a tennis court definitely can't give you a wet, slurpy kiss when you're having a bad day.

Chase told me I could come visit him in Hollywood. I told him he could come to my house if he wanted to try life as a normal kid. There was always plenty of food . . . but he might have to help with the dishes.

When we finished eating, we had to clean up every last crumb.  No one was supposed to bring food into the laboratory set. We even got down on our hands and knees to clean the floor.

Under the table, I found something: a long piece of pink plastic, with two silver gears attached to one end. There was a smudged black fingerprint in one corner.

"What's this?" I muttered.

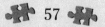

"The pig!" Chase yelped. "At least, a piece of it."

I took a closer look at the plastic piece. If it really broke off of the Axelrod Antimatter Electro-Grav-Matic, it was an important clue.

But it left us with an even bigger question:

Who broke it?

Chapter Ten
Making It Up

Chase rubbed the black fingerprint. "This is stage makeup," he said. "I'm supposed to wear it in my big scene with the pig."

I wondered who else wore black stage makeup. And I knew exactly who to ask.

We found Alicia in her trailer. She was watching TV.

Everything inside was pink. There were pink walls. A fluffy pink rug. Pink pillows on a pink couch. A giant mirror hanging over a pink makeup table, surrounded by pink lights.

I felt like I was trapped in a cotton candy machine.

"We have a question," I said. I showed Alicia the fingerprint. "Do you recognize this smudge?"

"Sure," she said. "That's Chase's makeup. He wears it on his face in the big pig scene."

"Does anyone else wear it?" I asked.

Alicia shook her head. Chase frowned. I knew what he was thinking. This was just another clue that led straight to one suspect — Chase Jackson. Everything pointed to him.

"Okay, kids!" she boomed, clapping her hands together. "It's four o'clock. I've gotta get going."

"It's four-twenty," Chase corrected her, glancing at his watch.

Alicia pointed at the clock on the wall. It was, of course, pink.

And it read four o'clock on the nose.

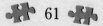

Chase held up his wrist. "This is a high-tech, waterproof, motion-powered watch. You can use it to check the weather. You can send e-mails with it. You can make phone calls with it. And you can *definitely* tell time with it. It's four-twenty."

I pulled out my pocket watch. It used to be my grandfather's. "Mine says the same thing," I told Alicia. "Four-twenty."

"Oh, no!" Alicia cried. "My clock batteries must be running low. No wonder I'm always late — I have to run!" She raced out of the trailer.

"Alicia said Hunter was with her when the pig was stolen," I mused. "But if her clock was wrong . . ."

"Hunter's alibi doesn't work anymore!" Chase exclaimed.

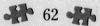

Chapter Eleven
The Big Break

Hunter Stone didn't have a fancy trailer. He and his mother were staying in an old RV, parked on the edge of the set. They had driven it all the way from Hollywood. We knocked on the door.

There was no answer.

Chase gave the door a small push. It swung open. "Hello?" I called. We stepped inside.

The RV was crammed with stuff. I couldn't believe Hunter and his mother lived inside. It was smaller than my bedroom!

Chase snatched up a stack of paper. "This is a script for my scene in the secret lab," he said. "I don't get it. Hunter isn't in this scene."

I ignored him. I was staring at a tiny piece of black fabric. It was caught on a nail, sticking out from the door frame. I slipped it into a plastic bag. I remembered Chase's black pants with the tear in the cuff.

"Chase, how did you tear your costume a few days ago?" I asked.

"*I* didn't tear it," he said. "I don't know how it got ripped."

I wished Mila were with us. I had all the pieces I needed to solve the puzzle. But I couldn't figure out how they fit together.

"I think Hunter tore your costume," I said. "This piece of fabric proves that he had it."

"And if he had the costume . . ." Chase began.

". . . then he was the one wearing it on the security tape," I finished.

"Jigsaw's right. It was me," said a small voice. The RV's door swung open. Hunter stood in the doorway, clutching the broken pig. He looked down at his feet. "I was pretending that *I* was the big star. I wanted to see what it was like to be the star by acting out a scene. So I put on Chase's costume and snuck into the prop room."

"But why did you break the pig?" I asked.

"I didn't *mean* to break the pig," Hunter said. "It was an accident. I didn't want to get you in trouble, Chase. I was scared."

"Scared of what?" I asked.

"Of getting kicked off the show," Hunter confessed. "I've only been in three episodes. I love being on TV. I want to be a star, more than anything. Just like Chase. He's . . . he's my hero."

Chase looked surprised. "I'm your hero?"

Hunter nodded.

Chase grinned. He clapped Hunter on the back. "Then I guess it's time for me to save the day."

Chapter Twelve
When Pigs Fly

The new star of *Spy Guy* stretched out in the sun. One of his assistants adjusted his sunglasses. Another one cooled him off with a giant fan. And a third held a bowl of ice water up to his mouth.

"I've never seen anyone so lazy and spoiled," I muttered.

He stared me right in the face.

And barked.

"I still can't believe you got Rags a part on the show," I told Chase. Rags wagged his tail. He loved the attention.

"I wanted to thank you," Chase said. He ruffled the soft fur on Rags's head.

Once we discovered the truth, Chase went with Hunter to confess to the director. They made sure that Les understood it was an accident. They even came up with an idea for a new scene with the broken pig. Hunter and Chase would search for the Axelrod Antimatter Electro-Grav-Matic together. But as soon as they found it, a

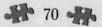

big, clumsy dog would run through the lab — and break it!

Guess who was playing the dog?

"I owe you one," Chase continued. "Especially since I'm the one getting all the credit." It was true. Every few minutes, someone came over to say, "Great job, Chase!"

I shrugged. "I don't need any credit," I told him. "Real detectives aren't in it for the glory. We just care about solving the case."

Those dollar bills in my back pocket didn't hurt, either.

Chase fed Rags a dog biscuit. In return, Rags gave him a sloppy kiss.

"So, how did you like being on TV?" Chase asked me.

"It was okay." I looked down at Rags, who was slurping ice water. At least one of us was enjoying the star treatment. "I'll be

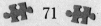

glad when things get back to normal. After all, I'm just a regular guy."

"You *really* don't want to be a star?" Chase asked. He couldn't believe it.

"Let Rags be the star. He likes the attention. *I'm* a detective," I said firmly. "And you can't teach an old dog new tricks."

"*Woof, woof!*" Rags agreed.

About the Author

James Preller often draws upon his own life as a basis for his Jigsaw Jones books. Like Jigsaw, James Preller has a slobbering, sock-eating dog. Like Jigsaw, James was the youngest in a large family. His older brothers called him Worm and worse — yeesh! And so do Jigsaw's!

James and Jigsaw both love jigsaw puzzles, baseball, grape juice, and mysteries! But even though Jigsaw and James have so much in common, they are not the same person.

Unlike Jigsaw, James Preller is the author of many books for children. He lives in Delmar, New York, with his wife, Lisa, his three kids — Nicholas, Gavin, and Maggie — his two cats, and his dog.

Learn more at www.jamespreller.com